SIMON & SCHUSTER BOOKS FOR YOUNG READERS
Simon & Schuster Building, Rockefeller Center,
1230 Avenue of the Americas, New York, New York 10020
Text copyright © 1988 by Maggie Davis
Illustrations copyright © 1988 by John Sandford
All rights reserved including the right of reproduction in
whole or in part in any form.
SIMON & SCHUSTER BOOKS FOR YOUNG READERS
is a trademark of Simon & Schuster Inc.
Manufactured in the United States of America.

10 9 8 7 6 5 4 3 2 1

(pbk) 10 9 8 7 6 5 4 3 2 1

Library of Congress Cataloging-in-Publication Data
Davis, Maggie S., 1942 – The rinky-dink cafe / by Maggie S. Davis. p. cm. Summary: An
insatiable pig marches into a restaurant that advertises "Dinners Made to Order" and demands
an amazing and amusing variety of dishes. ISBN 0-671-66408-5 [I. Pigs – Fiction.   2.
Food – Ficiton.]   I. Title. PZ7.D2952R in   1988[E] – dc19   87-35435   CIP   AC

ISBN: 0-671-66408-5   ISBN: 0-671-73621-3 (pbk)

For my mother
M.S.D.

Made to order for
Rick and Deann
J.S.

The Rinky-dink Café

By
Maggie S. Davis

Illustrated by
John Sandford

Simon and Schuster Books for Young Readers   Published by Simon & Schuster Inc.

New York

Into the Rinky-dink Café
marched Piggy La Puffin on Thanksgiving Day.
Cook waved from the kitchen. Waitress did, too.
"Have a seat," they called sweetly. "We're tasting a stew."

Piggy sat. Then she saw—in a crooked black border—
a large sign that read: WE MAKE DINNERS TO ORDER.

"It's true," grinned the waitress. "Ah," Piggy sighed.
"Then bring me cod soup and hot cider," she cried,
"and a bucket of clams caught near Old Plymouth Rock.
Could you serve up the clams in a pumpkin-shaped crock?"
"Don't know," said the waitress. "I'll go and ask Cook."
And ask him she did.

Well, Cook flashed a look that made poor Waitress fret.
His face was as gloomy as faces can get.
"I'm feeling blue," he moaned, checking the order.
"Darn that old sign with the crooked black border!"

"Something else?" asked the waitress. "You bet," Piggy said.
"A platter of oysters and fresh homebaked bread.
Some sliced beef with mustard, plus grapes—just a tad—
and corn that was picked by an Indian lad.
Serve it all on a garland of red and gold leaves.
Then, of course, a container of bread pudding, please."
"*My, my!*" said the waitress. "I'll go and tell Cook."
And tell him she did.

Well, Cook flashed a look that made poor Waitress dizzy.
He rolled and he bounced and he flew in a tizzy.
"I'm feeling weird," he wailed, waving the order.
"Let's rip up that sign with the crooked black border!"

"Something else?" asked the waitress, hefting the food.
"Right you are," Piggy said, " 'cause I'm in the mood
for sizzling plum porridge and turkey and dressing
and turnips and dumplings—I know I'm just guessing,
but do you have apples and steaming mince pies
that were baked by a child who can cross both his eyes?
Barrels of cranberries—that would be dandy—
and armfuls of cherries, and trays of nut candy,
and—"
"Stop!" said the waitress. "I'll go and tell Cook."
And tell him she did.

Well, Cook flashed a look that made poor Waitress sick.
He turned rosy red, beat the air with a stick.
"I'm feeling fierce!" he shrieked, spearing the order.
"I'll *eat* that old sign with the crooked black border!"

From the kitchen came shouts of "I wish I were dead!"
Piggy ignored them. She hummed and she read.
Waitress came out. Steam rose from her wig.
She looked older and wilder. "You ungrateful pig!"
were the words that she said as she wielded her tray.
"Could you bring me more food?" Piggy asked. "Right away?"

Just at that moment a shocking surprise—
the tray teetertottered. Despite Piggy's cries,
huge pots of goop tumbled down on her head.
When Piggy complained, Waitress scowled and she said:

"I'll forget that our restaurant is flooded with trash.
I'll forget you owe Cook and me buckets of cash.
I'll forget you aged each of us forty-three years,
that our Thanksgiving customers left here in tears.
But if you want sand that a pilgrim child played in,
more turkey, more cider, or even one raisin,
do not come to me with what you're proposing.
I'm pooped. Cook's on strike. What's more, dearie, we're *closing!*"

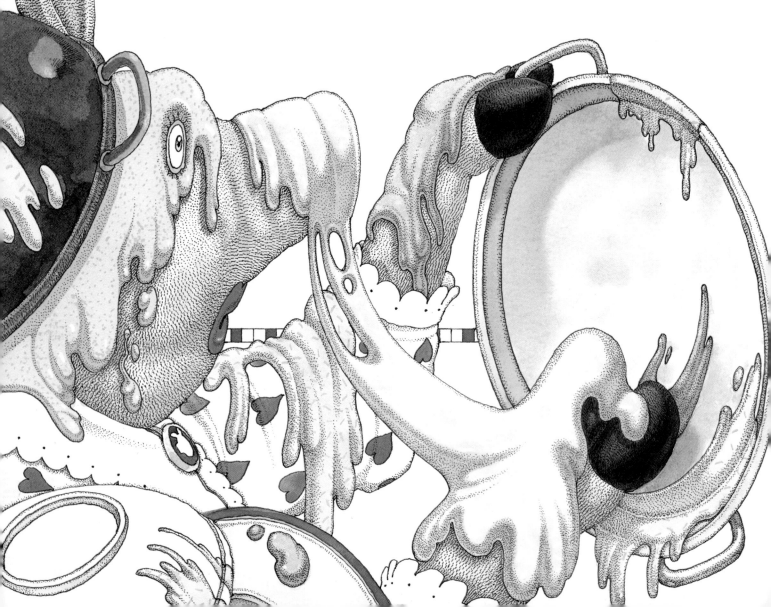

"Hmm," Piggy said, "I enjoyed your fine dinner
but dare say, I'm stuck here till I can get thinner."
Well, Waitress saw stars— couldn't take any more.
She called Cook: "Let's try pushing that pig out the door!"
"Whoa!" Piggy said. "I know what I'll do.
While I'm getting thin, I'll fix dinner for you!"
Waitress was tickled. Cook seemed pleased, too.
They waited politely till Piggy was through.

Then they ate every morsel she put on their plates.

Piggy tidied and scrubbed. In no time, she'd lost weight.

"Oh, thank you," Cook trilled. "We loved our Thanksgiving, dear—"
"Me, too!" said Piggy. "I'll come back next year!"